Mr. Maxwell's Mouse

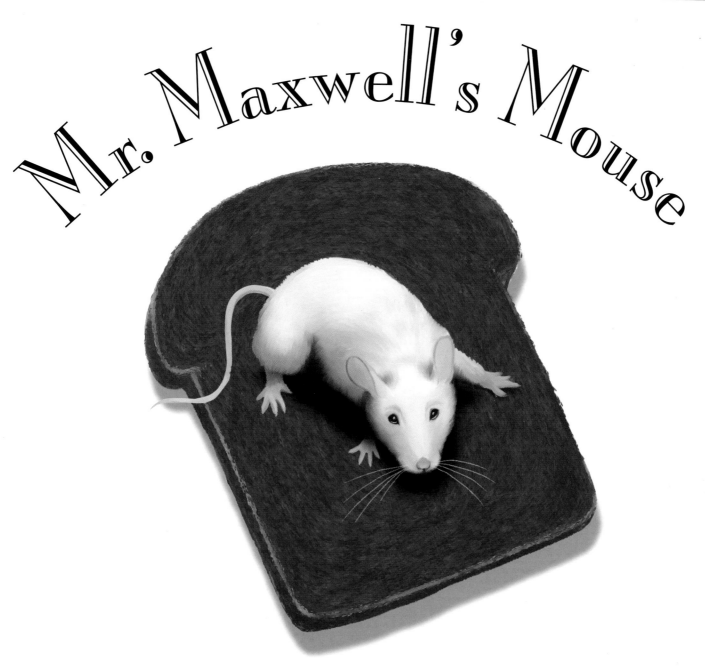

WRITTEN BY

ILLUSTRATED BY

Frank Asch   Devin Asch

KIDS CAN PRESS

First paperback edition 2014

Text © 2004 Frank Asch   Illustrations © 2004 Devin Asch

Kids Can Press acknowledges the financial support of the Government of Ontario, through the Ontario Media Development Corporation's Ontario Book Initiative.

Published in Canada by
Kids Can Press Ltd.
25 Dockside Drive
Toronto, ON M5A 0B5

Published in the U.S. by
Kids Can Press Ltd.
2250 Military Road
Tonawanda, NY 14150

www.kidscanpress.com

Kids Can Press is a *corus*™ Entertainment company

The artwork in this book was rendered in Adobe Photoshop and Corel Painter. The text is set in Celeste.

Edited by Tara Walker
Designed by Devin Asch and Karen Powers

The hardcover edition of this book is smyth sewn casebound.
The paperback edition of this book is limp sewn with a drawn-on cover.
Manufactured in Tseung Kwan O, NT Hong Kong, China, in 10/2013 by Paramount Printing Co. Ltd.

CM 04 0 9 8 7 6
CM PA 14 0 9 8 7 6 5 4 3 2 1

Library and Archives Canada Cataloguing in Publication

Asch, Frank
Mr. Maxwell's mouse / written by Frank Asch ; illustrated by Devin Asch.

ISBN 978-1-55337-486-2 (bound)   ISBN 978-1-77138-117-8 (pbk.)

1. Cats — Juvenile fiction. 2. Mice — Juvenile fiction.
3. Problem solving — Juvenile fiction. 4. Picture books for children.
I. Asch, Devin II. Title. III. Title: Mister Maxwell's mouse.

PS3551.S28M7 2004   j813'.54   C2003-907130-8

To Ada and Zoe

— F.A. & D.A.

Today, as usual, Mr. Howard Maxwell entered the Paw and Claw restaurant and was greeted by the headwaiter, Clyde.

"Good afternoon, sir," said Clyde with a gracious bow.

"Good afternoon, indeed!" replied Mr. Maxwell. "It isn't every day one is promoted to Vice Manager of Efficiency Control at Taylor, Bentwell and Nipson."

"Congratulations, sir," said Clyde, and he led Mr. Maxwell to his table.

Mr. Maxwell was the most regular regular at the Paw and Claw. Five days a week, rain or shine, he arrived at precisely 12:45, sat at the same table near the potted spider plant, and ordered baked mouse for lunch.

But today he asked for the menu.

"I'll have a mixed green salad for an appetizer," he announced, tapping his well-manicured claws on the arm of his chair. "And the raw mouse for my entrée."

"Excellent choice, sir. Would you like us to kill it for you?" asked Clyde.

"That won't be necessary," said Mr. Maxwell, noticing that the spider plant needed to be watered. "Just make sure it's fresh and healthy."

"All our mice are fresh and healthy," asserted Clyde. "And bred for plumpness and politeness as well!"

"I'm sure they are," said Mr. Maxwell as he closed his menu with a flourish.

While Mr. Maxwell ate his appetizer, he gloated over his promotion.

I wonder if my new office will have a picture window, he mused. *And it would be nice if there was a sofa where clients could sit and wait for me to notice them ...*

Clyde arrived with the main course just as Mr. Maxwell finished his salad.

"Your entrée, sir," said Clyde.

"Perfect timing," purred Mr. Maxwell. "I wish some of our employees at Taylor, Bentwell and Nipson were half so efficient!"

Clyde lifted the cover.

Mr. Maxwell's entrée was stretched out on a single slice of rye toast as if sunning itself on a sandy beach.

"Good afternoon, sir," said the mouse.

Mr. Maxwell's mouth began to water. *Good afternoon, indeed!* he thought.

"Aren't you going to add a little salt?" squeaked the mouse as Mr. Maxwell picked up his knife and fork.

Not having treated himself to a live mouse for a long time, Mr. Maxwell had grown unaccustomed to speaking with his meals.

"Ah ... yes ... thank you," he replied.

Soon the mouse felt fine crystals of salt pelting his fur and bouncing off his nose.

"Achoo!"

Looking up he saw that Mr. Maxwell was showering him with pepper as well as salt.

"Achoo! Achoo! Achoo!" the mouse sneezed until his nose was free of pepper.

"Gesundheit," said Mr. Maxwell.

"Thank you!" replied the mouse. "It's very comforting to know that I'm serving such a courteous customer."

Mr. Maxwell appreciated the compliment, but said nothing more. His mother had always advised him not to fraternize with his food.

Again Mr. Maxwell picked up his knife and fork.

"If I might be so bold ..." said the mouse as Mr. Maxwell was about to slice into his flesh. "May I ask one small favor?"

"That all depends," said Mr. Maxwell as he pressed the fork more firmly into the mouse's fur.

"I was just wondering if you wouldn't mind saying a little prayer before you ... begin," explained the mouse. "At home we always said a blessing before meals."

"Sorry, but I'm not at all religious," replied Mr. Maxwell.

"Oh, pardon me," said the mouse. "I hope you don't mind that I asked."

"Not at all," said Mr. Maxwell. "Will there be anything else?"

"Well ... actually there is," replied the mouse as he looked over the rim of his plate at the empty wine glass. "I always thought that when it was my turn to be ... ahem ... eaten, I would be enjoyed with a fine glass of wine."

"Sorry to disappoint you," said Mr. Maxwell. "Though
did receive a promotion today — more than just cause
or celebration — I never drink wine with lunch."

Mr. Maxwell instantly regretted telling the mouse
about his promotion.

"Congratulations on your good fortune, sir," said the
mouse. "I'm sure you'll do exceedingly well in your new
position. Perhaps someday you'll even become president
of your corporation."

"If I were you, I wouldn't be concerned with that right
now," said Mr. Maxwell. And to himself he thought, *What a
wordy mouse! I hope he doesn't give me indigestion.*

"Quite so," responded the mouse. "Say, would you mind
if I said a blessing for myself?"

Mr. Maxwell was tempted to end the conversation with
one quick thrust, but he eased back on his knife. "A prayer
would be acceptable. But make it short. I only have an hour
and a half for lunch."

"It will be a very short prayer," said the mouse, gently
pushing aside the fork. "Would you mind if I kneel?"

"You can stand on your head for all I care," hissed Mr.
Maxwell. "I just hope you're not entertaining any thoughts of
escape. This restaurant is full of cats. Even if you were shot
from a cannon, you wouldn't make it halfway to the door."

"Apparently you've never had a meal as well bred as myself!" the mouse bristled. "Allow me to assure you, sir, I have no desire to escape my fate."

As the mouse knelt beside the now cold slice of rye toast, Mr. Maxwell was reminded of a small kitten saying its bedtime prayers.

"Dear Lord," began the mouse. "Thank you very much for the wholesome upbringing I've had and the great honor of feeding this fine gentleman. Thank you for the wonderful friends I made while waiting in the pantry for my turn to serve catkind. Please bless Melissa, Pearl, Vera, Wilbur and especially tiny Albert, who wishes you would put some weight on him soon so he does not have to wait so long for his turn. I will miss them all. And please bless my dear mother and father and my many brothers and sisters, wherever they may be — dead or alive. They were all so good to me!" Suddenly the mouse choked up and a tiny tear appeared at the corner of his eye. As if embarrassed by this show of emotion, he abruptly ended his prayer with a quick "Amice!"

Slowly and with great dignity the mouse climbed back onto the toast and announced that he was ready.

Just then Clyde stepped over and asked, "Is everything all right, sir?"

"Yes, Clyde, everything is fine," replied Mr. Maxwell. "But perhaps I will have a glass of wine with my mouse after all."

"Why, of course!" said Clyde. "I have our wine list right here."

"I've heard that this year's Beaujolais is exceptional, but shamefully overpriced," offered the mouse. "So I'd suggest one of the fine Rhine wines — anything between the years '78 to '85, but not the '83. That year produced a very bitter crop of grapes. Unless you prefer a white wine with mouse — then almost any chardonnay will do."

"That would be my exact recommendation," said Clyde. "Didn't I tell you our mice are the very best?"

"Impressive," said Mr. Maxwell. "Bring me the Beaujolais."

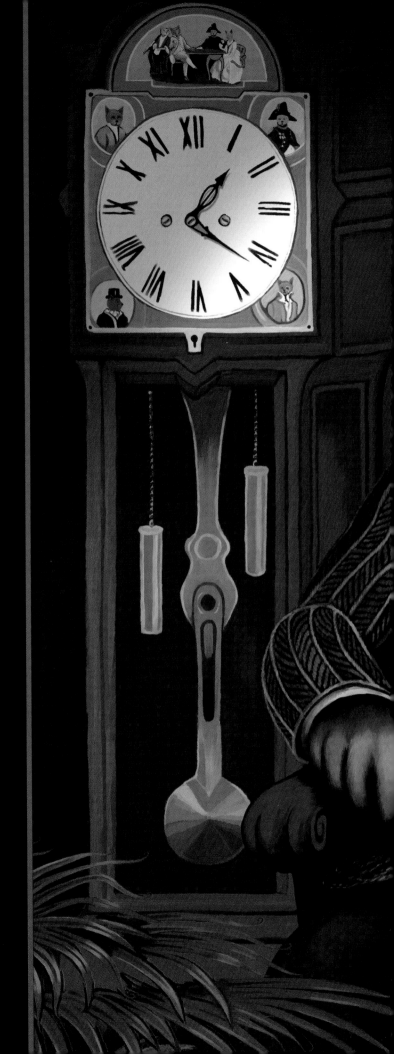

Mr. Maxwell sighed and looked down at his mouse in silence for a few moments.

"I know what you're thinking," said the mouse.

"Is that so?" said Mr. Maxwell.

"You're wondering if you should have chosen a Rhine wine instead," said the mouse.

"Actually I was wondering if I should ask the waiter to kill you for me," replied Mr. Maxwell.

"Oh, I'm terribly sorry," said the mouse. "I can see now that I've stepped over the line and become too personal with you. The chef warned repeatedly against doing that. Instead of making your meal more pleasant, I've made it more difficult! Please forgive me. This isn't easy for me either, you know."

"It's not your fault," Mr. Maxwell assured him. "It's just that I haven't had a live mouse in quite a while and ..."

"Then you must ask the waiter to help you out," insisted the mouse.

At that moment Clyde returned with the wine.

"Will there be anything else, sir?" he asked.

"No, thank you, Clyde," said Mr. Maxwell.

When Clyde was gone the mouse said, "I understand. You don't want to appear squeamish. It would not be catly."

"Quite the contrary. I have no concern for appearances in matters of this sort. I just thought you deserved to be dispatched by someone who, shall we say, knows you," said Mr. Maxwell, and he drank his wine in one long gulp. "I've had many live mice. When I was younger — dozens of them! But now I just can't seem to ..."

"I know I should be quiet right now," whispered the mouse. "But may I suggest you make a blindfold with your napkin? It will make it so much easier."

Mr. Maxwell picked up his knife and fork and set them down again. "No! I just can't!"

"But you *must*!" insisted the mouse. "You're a cat and I'm a mouse. Certain things cannot be changed. Please, try the blindfold."

"Perhaps I'm just getting older," said Mr. Maxwell as he tied his napkin tightly around his eyes. "My own death doesn't seem as far off as it used to ..." Mr. Maxwell's tail swished nervously back and forth.

"You can do this," said the mouse as he leaned over the edge of the table and gently grabbed hold of Mr. Maxwell's tail. "I know you can."

Mr. Maxwell's paws shook so much that his knife and fork began to rattle.

"Just steady your knife," instructed the mouse as he guided Mr. Maxwell's tail to the plate. "That's it. Now, when I count to three, thrust with all your might."

"Very well," said Mr. Maxwell with a deep sigh. "I just want to say one thing ... Thank you. Thank you very much. You've been most patient with me."

"No need to thank me," replied the mouse. "Just enjoy your meal. Ready? Here we go. One, two ..."

"I'm sorry about this," said Mr. Maxwell. "Really I am. It's nothing personal, you know."

"Likewise," said the mouse, and he called out, "THREE!"

OOOOOOO WWWW!

Mr. Maxwell's howl of pain was heard three blocks away at Taylor, Bentwell and Nipson. It was so powerful that the patrons near his table were knocked off their chairs. Clyde dropped a whole tray of boiled lobsters, and the chef spilled a pot of hot oil, setting the kitchen on fire.

In the mayhem no one noticed Mr. Maxwell's mouse race to the pantry and free all the other mice.

As mice scattered in every direction, an ambulance arrived to take Mr. Maxwell to the emergency room.

Mr. Maxwell's mouse has never been recaptured. Rumors linking him to other daring mouse escapes have spread far and wide. But thus far no proof of his definite whereabouts has surfaced.

Late one night, however, soon after the incident at the restaurant, a small handwritten note on lightly scented lavender paper was slipped under Mr. Maxwell's hospital door.

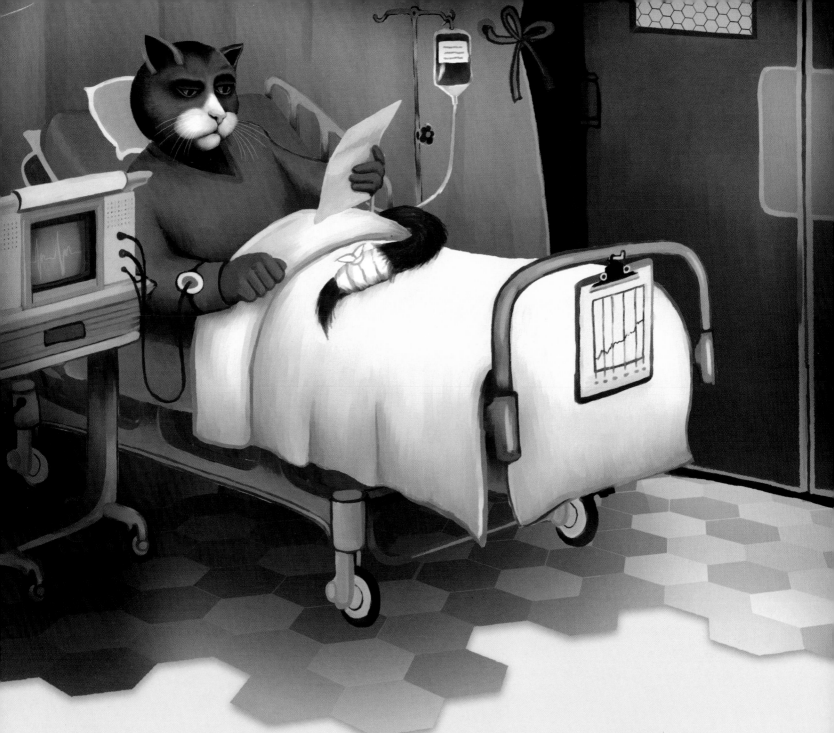

Dear Sir,

   I just want you to know that I sincerely regret any distress I may have caused you.
I'm sure you would have taken similar measures had you found yourself in my position.
Meanwhile I trust that you and your tail are well on the road to recovery. Of course I bear
you no ill will and can only imagine that you feel the same.

   May you live a long and prosperous life.

   Sincerely,

   Your friend from the Paw and Claw